ELLA AND THE NAUGHTY LION

written by

ANNE COTTRINGER

pictures by

RUSSELL AYTO

Houghton Mifflin Company
Boston 1996

TO: Raquel

The day Ella's mother
 came home with baby Jasper, a lion
 slipped in through the door.

He was a very naughty lion.

He pulled off Jasper's blanket.

He crept into Jasper's crib

and stretched out in a long yawn.
There was no room for Jasper.

When Ella's mother fed Jasper, the lion roared
so loudly, the whole house shook.

The lion tore up Jasper's soft brown teddy

and then chewed it into little wet bits.

"Naughty lion," said Ella. "That was Jasper's favorite teddy! Don't you ever do that again!"

But sometimes the lion was a good lion.
When Ella's grandmother took Ella out
for the day, the lion went too.
He wasn't a naughty lion at all.

He slid down the slide with Ella.

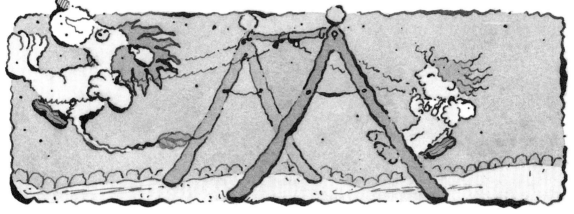

He swung on the swing.

He got dizzy from whizzing around the
merry-go-round with Ella and her friends.

But when they got home, the lion
jumped into Jasper's bath . . .

and splashed water
all over the bathroom.

The next day, Jasper had
the snuffles and couldn't get to sleep.
He was very grizzly.

Ella wanted her mother to
play zoo with her.

"I can't, Ella. I'm too busy
with Jasper," said her mother.

"Why don't you go to the supermarket
with Daddy and maybe he'll buy
something nice to eat!"

But Ella didn't want anything nice to eat.
She was very unhappy. So was the lion,
and he was naughtier than ever!

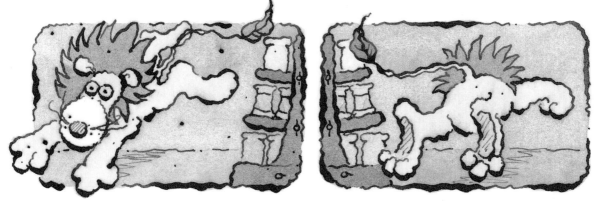

He galloped up and down the aisles.

He knocked over stacks of baked beans

and crashed through a pyramid of oranges.

He gobbled up some cakes and got pink icing
all over his whiskers.

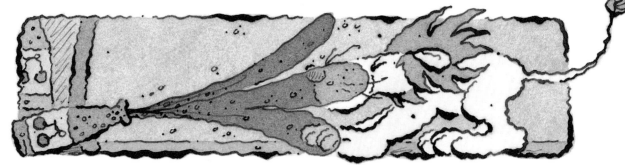

He spilled a big bottle of fizzy red cherry soda
that spurted like a fountain over everything

He roared so loudly that he frightened all
the people at the checkout.

"Bad, bad, bad lion!" Ella scolded him all the way home.
"Don't you ever behave like that again!"

When they got home,
Jasper was asleep in his carriage.
Ella's father squeezed past with
his shopping bags.

The naughty lion bounded on behind him and
bumped Jasper's carriage.

It started
to roll

towards the
open door,

and before
anyone
knew it,

the carriage
was bouncing
down the steps.

Ella and the lion watched with wide eyes.
Then the lion roared a big roar.

In a flash, Ella leaped
and caught hold of Jasper as
he sailed through the air.

Ella's mother and father rushed out.
"Oh Ella! What would we do
without you!" cried her mother.
"Well done," said her father.
The lion growled deep down
inside his throat.

Ella's mother
made some
hot chocolate.

Ella sat on the sofa
with Jasper gurgling
happily in her arms.
Ella smiled at her
baby brother and
gave his rattle
a little shake.

The lion got a
very grumpy look
on his face.
He flicked his
tail back and forth,
but Ella didn't notice.

And so the lion
slipped out just as
he had come in.

But from time to
time Ella heard a little
growl at the door.

Walter Lorraine (w£) Books

Text copyright © 1996 by Anne Cottringer
Illustrations copyright © 1996 by Russell Ayto
First American edition 1996
Originally published in Great Britain in 1996
by William Heinemann Ltd, an imprint of Reed Consumer Books Limited
All rights reserved. For information about permission to reproduce
selections from this book, write to Permissions, Houghton Mifflin Company,
215 Park Avenue South, New York, New York 10003.
For information about this and other Houghton Mifflin trade and reference books and multimedia
products, visit The Bookstore at Houghton Mifflin on the World Wide Web at
http://www.hmco.com/trade/.

Library of Congress Cataloging-in-Publication Data

Cottringer, Anne.
Ella and the naughty lion / written by Anne Cottringer;
illustrated by Russell Ayto. – 1st American ed.
p. cm.
Summary: The day Ella's mother comes home with baby Jasper,
a lion slips through the door and takes up residence with the family,
disturbing everyone with its naughty behavoir.
ISBN 0–395–79753–5 (hardcover)
[1. Brothers and sisters – Fiction. 2. Lions – Fiction.] I. Ayto,
Russell, ill. II. Title.
PZ7.C82967E1 1996
[E]–dc20
95–53271
CIP
AC

Printed in Hong Kong

10 9 8 7 6 5 4 3 2 1